SCOOBY-DOO!

and the

Phantom Prankster

SCOOBY-DOO!

and the

Phantom Prankster

Written by Jo Hurley

SCHOLASTIC INC.

New York Toronto London Auckland Sydney

Mexico City New Delhi Hong Kong Buenos Aires

ISBN 0-439-73708-7

Designed by Joseph R. Williams

12 11 10 9 8 7 6 5 4 3 2 1   5 6 7 8 9/0

Printed in the U.S.A.
First printing, April 2005

Chapter 1

"Like, this hero needs more hot sauce," Shaggy said as he shook a jar of Totally Tamale onto his super-sized salami sandwich.

"Rum Rum!" Scooby licked his lips and leaned in for a taste. His stomach growled as he bit into one end and Shaggy bit the other end.

"How can you two eat at a time like this?" Velma groaned. "Daphne and her Uncle Walt need our help."

"Like, there's always time for eating, see?" Shaggy

said, swallowing half his sandwich in one bite.

They were on their way to visit Daphne's Uncle Walt in Quaky Ridge. His joke store, the Giggle Spot, had been in the family for over a century, and now it looked like it might have to close. A new joke shop, the Laugh Arcade, had just opened across the street, and it was muscling in on Uncle Walt's business.

In order to boost business, Uncle Walt was hosting a huge birthday bash for the mayor's son and everyone important in town was coming. Daphne promised that she and the Mystery, Inc. gang would be on hand to help out.

Now the gang was off to Quaky Ridge — Fred loaded up the Mystery Machine with everyone's sleeping bags and suitcases, and Shaggy made sure the traveling mini-fridge was stocked.

After two hours, the gang finally arrived at their destination. A neon sign inside the window of Uncle Walt's store flashed: THE JOKE STOPS HERE, and the window was crammed with goofy disguises and masks, feather boas, and other funny stuff.

"Like, it looks like the circus exploded in there,"

Shaggy said peering in through the window.

"It always looked that way," Daphne said, "Ever since I was a little kid."

Across the street was the Laugh Arcade, a much bigger joke store with gleaming steel and sparkling glass windows. Unlike the small, crowded windows at Walt's shop, the Laugh Arcade windows showcased seven-foot rubber chickens and huge flies with green wings.

"Jinkies! That store is enormous!" Velma cried.

"That must be the Laugh Arcade, the place that's stealing all of Uncle Walt's customers," Daphne said.

Chapter 2

Daphne, Velma, Fred, Scooby, and Shaggy stood on the sidewalk in front of Uncle Walt's store looking across the street at the giant Laugh Arcade. Dozens of people walked into the super store, but no one entered the Giggle Spot.

"Hmmmm," Fred rubbed his chin thoughtfully. "I wonder what makes that place so much more popular than Walt's store?"

Just then a little boy and his father walked up to the Laugh Arcade.

"Why don't we ask those two?" Daphne suggested.

Velma approached the man and the boy. "Excuse me," she asked, "Can you tell me why you're shopping at the Laugh Arcade rather than the Giggle Spot?"

"Why certainly," the man replied, "The quality at the Giggle Spot just isn't what it used to be. Everyone's been talking about it — I heard that last week some Giggle Spot stay-lit candles malfunctioned at a birthday party and the entire cake exploded! I wouldn't want to risk anything like that happening at our party! That's why I'm going to choose the Laugh Arcade from now on, for all my joke shop needs."

As the man and his son walked through the automatic doors to the Laugh Arcade, the sound of laughter was piped out onto the street through a speaker system.

"Row! Rexroding Rake!" Scooby exclaimed.

"Yeah Scoob, like I'm with you," Shaggy said licking his lips, "I'll take an explosion any day, as long as it's exploding cake!"

Everyone turned back toward the dusty, dark

entrance to the Giggle Spot. They had to admit that it looked less enticing then the shiny brand-new windows of the Laugh Arcade.

"Let's not come to any conclusions until we've talked to Uncle Walt and had a look around his store for ourselves," Daphne said.

Uncle Walt came out of his shop to greet the Mystery, Inc. gang. He hugged Daphne, who introduced Fred, Velma, Shaggy, and Scooby.

"Scooby-Dooby-Doo!" Scooby said, holding out his paw.

Uncle Walt chuckled.

"I said my business was going to the dogs, but I never expected a real one would show up to help me out."

Everyone laughed as they went inside Uncle Walt's store.

"By the way, there's something else I didn't tell you on the phone, Daphne," Uncle Walt said. "I'm not just losing business these days. I think someone has been stealing from my stockroom."

"Do you know who it is?" Fred asked.

Uncle Walt shook his head. "No, I don't know who it is. But I realized this morning that I'm missing a new shipment of itching powder and stay-lit candles."

"We'll get to the bottom of everything, Uncle Walt. I promise," Daphne said.

"Can you start with him?" Walt said. He indicated a large man now standing in front of the Giggle Spot. The man wore a dark suit. He peered in through the windows and glared at the gang through a pair of thick glasses as he puffed on his cigar.

"Like, that's one serious looking dude!" Shaggy said.

"Rooks rike rubble!" Scooby said.

"Yeah, Scoob, he does look like trouble," Daphne said.

"Well, don't look now but it looks like trouble's coming our way," Fred said as the man walked through the swinging doors and into the store.

"Hello there, kids!" the man yelled as he approached the group. "Is this a meeting of the Giggle Spot fan club or what?"

"And who, may I ask, are you?" Velma asked.

"Ebenezer Bleezer's the name," the man said. "I'm the owner of the Laugh Arcade. And who are you?"

"We're friends of Walt," Fred said, suspiciously eyeing Bleezer.

"We're detectives," Velma said.

"Do you detect a little slump in Walt's business?" Bleezer said. He laughed so loud it sounded like he had stereo speakers in his suit.

"Very funny, Bleezer," Walt said.

"Well, business is just BOOMING for me these days!" Bleezer bellowed. "Why don't you and your kids stop over at the Arcade? You might learn something."

"No thanks," Walt said. "I've told you before. You don't run my kind of joke shop."

"You know, Walt, the only joke around here is your lack of customers," Bleezer said with another loud laugh.

"Now, just a minute!" Daphne said, grabbing Uncle Walt's arm protectively. "You don't know what you're talking about, Mr. Bleezer. The Giggle Spot is planning a major shindig…"

"That's guaranteed to bring in tons of customers," Fred added.

"Like, it's being catered," Shaggy said.

"Reah," Scooby said. "Rummy!"

"In fact, Even the mayor will be attending," Velma said.

"The MAYOR? Fiddlesticks!" Bleezer laughed loudly. He stomped out his cigar at Walt's feet and then walked back across the street toward his arcade.

"Fiddlesticks?" Shaggy asked. "Like, is that some kind of new snack food?"

"Hey guys, check out what I just found!" Fred called the gang over to him, and they all looked at a crumpled piece of paper he had just picked up off the floor.

"Rut ruz it ray?" Scooby asked?

Velma read it out loud:

"Warning! The Giggle Spot sells unsafe and

cheap merchandise. For real quality pranks, head across the street to the Laugh Arcade. This…" Fred trailed off.

"Like what's the rest of it say?" Shaggy asked.

"I don't know, it looks like the rest of it's ripped off," Velma said. "Something definitely fishy is going on and it's a good thing we're here to get to the bottom of it."

Chapter 3

"What's wrong with that clock?" Fred said as they walked through the doors of the Giggle Spot.

Up on the wall was a large black-and-white clock that seemed perfectly normal except that the numbers were backward.

Uncle Walt laughed. "I've got all sorts of gag clocks around here," he said. "Clocks that glow, vibrate, and even scream."

"Zoinks!" exclaimed Shaggy.

"That sure is a good clock for a practical joker," Fred said.

"According to my research, modifying a common object like

a clock to fool its user is one of the most common practical jokes," Velma explained.

"It was one of my best sellers," Walt groaned. "Before Bleezer came along."

Uncle Walt gave the gang a quick tour of the front store before disappearing into the back office. He needed to make a few last-minute calls before the party.

As soon as Walt was out of sight, Fred pulled Daphne aside. "I think your Uncle's in serious trouble, Daph," he said. "That Bleezer guy really seems to know what he's doing."

"Don't say that, Freddy," Daphne said. "Bleezer's just a big bully. We'll be able to help Uncle Walt turn his business around."

"Let's take a look around the shop before the party starts," suggested Velma.

Scooby and Shaggy were already getting acquainted. Scooby had found a big bin with a sign that said: DO NOT TOUCH. Underneath that in smaller letters it said: JUST KIDDING. In the bin was a giant hot dog in a bun.

"Rummy! Rummy! Rummy!" Scooby called out. He started to drool.

Shaggy heard him and ran over with a red plastic bottle of ketchup that he'd found on another counter.

"Snacktime!" Shaggy said. He aimed the ketchup at the hot dog and squeezed. White stuff shot out like silly string. Scooby was covered.

"Sorry Scoob," Shaggy snickered. "Like, that wasn't supposed to happen."

There were pranks everywhere. Fred found a big boulder made of foam and lifted it over his head pretending to be super strong. Daphne found a mirror that let out a ghoulish laugh whenever she looked at it. Shaggy fell for a rubber hand with fingers that moved. Velma even found a book called *The Secrets of the Tse-Tse Fly* that was actually a safe where she could hide valuables, like her extra pairs of glasses.

Scooby found the best prank of all—a small camera with a Velcro strap that fit over his paw. Instead of taking real photographs, this camera squirted water.

Daphne led the way to the back of the store. It was like an amusement park fun house with winding hallways leading to darkened rooms.

"The best part about Walt's shop is all these secret rooms and passages," Daphne said, " I always got lost in here when I was younger."

Fred opened one unlocked door and a bat flew out.

"Eeeeeeek!" Velma cried as the bat flew around her head. Scooby shrieked, too, and jumped into Shaggy's arms.

"Wait! That's not a real bat," Daphne said, grabbing it in midair. "Uncle Walt always triggered gags throughout his store. That's just one of his favorites, the flying rubber bat."

"Check this out," Velma said, poking her nose into another room. There were half-opened crates marked with bright, glowing green letters. One said EXPLODING CIGARS. Another read FAKE ANTS. Along one wall was a sign that read STAY-LIT CANDLES but there were no boxes under it.

"This must be Uncle Walt's main storage area," Fred said.

"And, like, that must be where the candles were stolen from!" Shaggy said.

"Rat's Right!" exclaimed Scooby.

Velma looked down at the ground and scratched her chin thoughtfully. "Hey, look at this," she said. On the ground in the dust was a piece of fuzzy purple material and a single french fry.

Shaggy and Scooby rushed over.

"RENCH RIE!" Scooby said.

"Like, Velma, maybe Scooby and I should hold on to that clue for safe keeping," Shaggy said.

"Not so fast, Shaggy," Velma said depositing the fry and the purple fuzz in her pocket. "Unless my glasses deceive me, it looks like we may have a clue to Uncle Walt's mystery thief," Velma said.

Chapter 4

After the gang had taken a tour of the store, it was time to get ready for the party.

Fred and Walt unloaded boxes and the rest of the gang hung streamers and decorations. The store had its CLOSED, PLEASE COME AGAIN sign on the front door so that they could get ready for the party. Suddenly the door opened and an angry-looking man walked into the shop. He was wearing a fuzzy purple sweater.

"Frank, what are you doing here?" Uncle Walt said with a gasp.

"Who is this guy?" Daphne asked her uncle.

"Most people call me Frank the Prank. I used to be the best darn prank salesman in this town, and now I'm just a lowly short order cook," he said with a sneer.

"I heard you're having a big party, Walt, but I didn't get an invitation."

"No, I didn't invite you Frank," Walt said. "I'm sorry. I thought it was best."

"That was a mistake," Frank growled, "You'll be sorry you ever met Frank the Prank!" Frank turned and stormed out of the store, nearly knocking over Scooby-Doo.

"RRIKES!" Scooby yowled.

"Jinkies!" Velma exclaimed. "What's the matter with him?"

"Frank used to work here at the store. He's a whiz at practical jokes, but he wasn't very friendly with my customers, so I had to let him go." Walt explained.

"Wait!" Shaggy suddenly exclaimed, wildly sniffing the air. "Scoob! Like, do you smell what I smell!"

Scooby already had his nose to the ground sniffing out where Frank the Prank had stood only moments before.

"Rench Ries!" Scooby cried out.

"Hmm...," Velma said scratching her head. "We found a french fry in the stock room... there's definitely something strange going on... hey, what have you got there Scooby?"

Scooby had sniffed out a scrap of paper, and Fred took it from him and read it.

"It says, 'flyer good for one free hand buzzer at the Laugh Arcade.'"

"That must be the rest of the flyer that we found after Bleezer left!" Daphne said.

Fred pulled the piece of the flyer out of his pocket and put the new scrap in place. He read the whole thing.

"Warning! The Giggle spot sells unsafe and cheap merchandise. For real quality pranks, head across the street to the Laugh Arcade. This flyer good for one free hand buzzer at the Laugh Arcade."

"Like, someone's trying to scare people away from the Giggle Spot!" Shaggy said

"Reah!" Scooby barked in agreement.

"Well, gang," Velma said, "It looks to me like we've got a mystery to solve."

"Yeah, like, just as soon as this birthday bash is over!" Shaggy said looking up at the many people lined up outside the doors of the Giggle Spot waiting for the party to begin.

As the guests filed into the Giggle Spot, TV news cameras and reporters milled around, trying to get interviews with local celebrities. Scooby and Shaggy stopped mugging for the cameras long enough to notice a big sign on the Laugh Arcade door that read CLOSED.

"So, like, I guess we don't have to worry about Ebenezer Bleezer trying to steal Walt's customers today." Shaggy said.

But just when all the guests had made it inside, a big commotion could be heard outside the store.

"Down with the Giggle Spot! Pranks are for punks!" shouted a group of protesters.

Their leader was a woman dressed in a long black coat with a fuzzy purple wool scarf wrapped around her neck. She stared directly into one of the TV cameras.

"I'm Polly Cracker, head librarian in Quaky Ridge. Every week, kids play pranks in my library. Last week it was gluing together the pages of the dictionary. This week it was a whoopee cushion on my seat! We want the Giggle Spot closed — NOW!"

"Down with the Giggle Spot! Close this store no matter what!" Polly yelled. The other protesters joined in.

"Oh, Daphne," Uncle Walt sighed. "I sure am glad

you kids are here. I don't know what I would do if you hadn't come."

"Don't worry, Uncle Walt," Daphne said gently. "Everything will work out."

"Like, your store is the grooviest," Shaggy said.

The sound of music filled the air. The clown band had finally arrived and they were tuning up. Uncle Walt's spirits lifted a little. The music would drown out the voices of Polly and any other picketers. Now the party could really get rocking!

Shaggy and Scooby watched the clowns set up their band equipment. There were clowns with big yellow shoes, red noses, and funny hats with propellers on top. One carried a tuba. Another one put together a brightly colored drum set. Another clown was wearing a big, fluffy, purple wig and black glasses — he didn't have an instrument.

"Hey Scoob, like, check out that clown, will ya? I wonder where his instrument is." Shaggy said as the clown in the purple wig left the rest of the band and walked through a door marked EMPLOYEES ONLY.

As they were talking, a waiter passed by them

with a tray of half-eaten snacks. He headed toward the kitchen through a pair of swinging doors.

Scooby's stomach grumbled.

"Forget those clowns! Follow the food!" Shaggy said, as the two of them snuck into the kitchen behind the waiter.

Chapter 5

"Raggy? Rello?" Scooby asked. It was almost pitch black inside the back of the store.

"Like, where did that waiter go? I know I smell snacks around here somewhere," Shaggy said, sniffing.

"Reepers," Scooby said. "Rit's releee rark rere."

The back area of the store seemed deserted. Its passages and storage rooms seemed a little scarier than it had the night before.

"Um . . . maybe we should go back to the party?" Shaggy suggested.

Scooby agreed, but they didn't know where to

turn next — they were stuck inside the maze of halls and rooms.

"Do you smell that?" Shaggy asked.

Scooby drooled. "Reah, Reah!" It smelled like french fries.

The pair crept along in the dark in search of food. The sounds of the party had died down now, and it was so quiet that Shaggy could hear the squeak of his own basketball sneakers and Scooby's paws padding next to him. But there was another sound too: Clop, slap. Clop, slap. Clop, slap.

"Um…Scoob, do you like get the feeling we're being followed?" Shaggy asked.

"Rollowed?" Scooby gulped.

They stopped walking. The footsteps stopped, too. Slowly, they turned around.

"Aaaaaaaah!"

Scooby and Shaggy found themselves face to face with the clown in the purple wig!

Shaggy grabbed Scooby's paw and ran.

The clown chased them into a crooked hallway and disappeared into the darkness.

"Ruck!" Scooby yelped as he looked down at his paws. There was sticky black stuff all over them.

"Like, this is one spooky scene!" Shaggy whispered. "That prankster is playing pranks on us!"

Shaggy and Scooby heard a loud laugh in the distance and then the familiar sound of clown shoes flapping. There was no time to loose. The prankster burst through a corridor and once again they were off. Scooby and Shaggy, dodged in and out of more rooms, tripping over boxes of gag gifts. They dashed past a giant inflatable skeleton hanging from the ceiling.

"Riiiiikes!" Scooby screamed

"Quick! In here!" Shaggy cried.

Scooby followed Shaggy into a room filled with crates. The only light on in the room was the dim red glow from an emergency exit sign. A cloud of white powder in the air blinded them both for a moment.

Scooby started to itch.

"Aw, Scoob, like this is no time to get an attack of the fleas," Shaggy cried.

But then he started to itch, too. In fact, they both

started itching and jumping around so much that they knocked over another crate.

"Ahhhhhh!" Shaggy cried. He looked down. There were ants everywhere.

"Rants!" Scooby cried. "RAAAAANTS!"

Shaggy and Scooby ran as fast as they could to

the emergency exit door. A sign on it read EMERGENCY ONLY!

"Like, Scoob, this looks like an emergency to me!" Shaggy said

"Roo raid it!" Scooby yelped as the two of them burst through the door into one of the party rooms.

"Hey you two! You look like you saw a ghost!" Velma cried.

"We're being chased by the c-c-clown in a purple wig!" Shaggy said.

Uncle Walt recognized the smell of powder on Shaggy's shirt. "Hey, that's my special scented itching powder," he said. "Were you two in my back room?"

"Yeah! And we were itching to get out of there!" Shaggy said.

"Ritching!" Scooby said, nodding and scratching at the same time.

"Hey Scoob, what's that stuck to your paw?" Fred asked as he pulled a folded up piece of paper off the black tar on Scooby's paw.

"That looks like a map of the Giggle Spot!" Velma said. "The clown must have dropped it when he was chasing you! Let's go tell Uncle Walt about this!"

Chapter 6

Daphne pushed her way through guests at the crowed party to get to her uncle who was talking to the mayor. Suddenly there was a loud noise, and a huge cloud of smoke filled the air, along with the distinct odor of skunks. Uncle Walt threw up his hands. "Someone's thrown a stink bomb!" he cried.

The mayor ducked and the crowd scattered as best they could in the packed store.

"That sure is one way to raise a stink!" Velma declared.

"Are you okay?" Walt asked the mayor.

The mayor sat in a chair. "I think so," he said, checking his toupee.

"Someone get me a drink for the mayor!" Walt said.

"Poor Uncle Walt," Daphne sighed. "We have to help calm down the crowd so no one leaves the party."

Scooby brought Walt a glass of punch from the refreshment table. The mayor was about to take a sip, when his jaw dropped.

"What is THIS?" the mayor cried.

Inside the red punch was a floating eyeball. Walt plucked it out of the glass. It was made of rubber — Daphne and Fred rushed over to check the punch bowl. There were even more eyeballs in it — and some flies in the ice cubes, too.

"Help! Help! HELP!" a voice cried.

"That sounds like my son!" the mayor said.

"The gumballs are toxic!" someone yelled.

One party guest said that his gumball tasted like pepper. Another gumball tasted like tuna fish. The mayor's son clutched his stomach, too. His gumball tasted like dirty socks!

"Someone must have substituted bad gumballs for the cherry-flavored ones we put into the machine this morning," Velma said.

The crowd squealed. The mayor yelled. The gang tried to calm everyone down.

"I came to this store to have a party for my son, not to get pranked!" the mayor said. "I'm taking back my endorsement for the Giggle Spot unless you've got a good explanation for what's going on."

"Mr. Mayor," Velma said, "We think whoever's been stealing from Uncle Walt's store is trying to sabatoge your party."

"Who are these kids?" the mayor pointed to Velma and asked Uncle Walt.

Fred took charge. "We're Mystery, Inc., Mr. Mayor.

And we're here to help Daphne's uncle save his store, and save your son's party."

"Oh, kids. It's too late. After this mess, I'm ruined," Uncle Walt said.

"I wouldn't throw in the towel just yet Uncle Walt," Daphne said.

"Daphne's right," Fred said, "Just leave it to Mystery, Inc. — we'll come up with a super plan to catch your prankster!"

"My intuition tells me that the prankster's not going anywhere until he's certain your store is history," Velma said. "In fact, he's probably still inside the store planning another prank. What we need to do is catch him in the act and beat him at his own game."

"That's right," Fred said, "Shaggy, Scooby — you're the ones who saw him last, so we'll need you two to go back to the stockroom to bring him out of hiding."

"H-h-hold on! Y-y-you mean we really have to g-g-go back there?" Shaggy sputtered. "Like, no way Jose!"

"How about if we gave you a Scooby Snack?" Velma

coaxed.

Shaggy's and Scooby's ears both perked up. "Like, now you're talking our language, right Scoob?" Shaggy said.

"Scooby Snack?" Scooby licked his chops. "Ruh-uh!"

Chapter 7

The clown band started up again, and the party resumed. The Mystery, Inc. gang was stationed in the back rooms of the Giggle Spot, and had decided to split up to cover more ground.

Velma retrieved her flashlight and went searching for the clown down one of

Uncle Walt's mysterious corridors. She found a room filled with giant fake tombstones with names like I.B. DEAD and REST IN PIECES. Giant cobwebs hung from the ceiling. Velma hoped there were no giant spiders living in here.

Scooby and Shaggy wandered through another hallway. In one teeny-tiny closet of a room, Shaggy discovered a bag of disguises. He put on a rubber nose and orange wig and grabbed a funny pair of yellow dotted pants and orange sneakers for Scooby. The two left the room dressed up looking like they were ready to join the clown band.

A little further down the dark hall, Shaggy spotted a table: it was piled high with cakes, candy and cookies.

"Like, pinch me Scoob, I must be dreaming!" Shaggy said.

"Rec roo!" Scooby said.

Shaggy grabbed a handful of chocolates. Scooby grabbed a cake.

"Reeeeech!" Scooby said, spitting out the cake.

"Ptoooooey!" Shaggy cried. He spit out his food, too. "That's plastic and cardboard. This food is fake!"

A deep, laugh came from the corner.

"Wh-wh-whoa!" Shaggy said. "Wh-wh-what was

that?"

Then he saw something lurking in the shadows. The purple clown!

Shaggy tried to run. His legs were moving fast but he was going nowhere — the purple clown had grabbed the back of his shirt.

Scooby tried to distract the clown by circling around and around the purple clown who looked very confused. Where did these other two clowns come from?

As soon as the purple clown was distracted, Shaggy and Scooby ran in the opposite direction down the hall as fast as their legs could take them. Velma, Daphne, and Fred were headed down the same hall.

Fred and Velma turned around. The purple clown was right there. He let out a laugh that sounded a lot more like a roar.

"That sounds strangely familiar," Velma said.

Everyone dashed for a different door. Scooby got up, too, but a piece of his clown costume was stuck to a nail on the floor.

"Zoinks!" Shaggy yelled. The purple clown glared

at him. Scooby held up his prank camera that he'd picked out the day before.

"Ray Reese!" Scooby said.

The clown stopped dead in his tracks and looked right at the camera as Scooby pressed the shutter.

Splurt!

Water came squirting out of the prank camera lens. The purple clown threw his hands up to his eyes and fell over his own, clunky clown shoes, right through an open door into a pile of boxes.

"Gee, Scoob," Daphne said with a smile. "Talk about a photo finish!"

"Ree, ree, ree," Scooby laughed.

The clown started to make a run for it, but Fred

stepped in and grabbed his clown suit. Uncle Walt had called the police, and they emerged from behind a door.

"Now let's see who the prankster really is!" Fred said.

Chapter 8

Uncle Walt, the mayor, and the Mystery, Inc. gang stood around the clown in the purple wig — the police had put him in handcuffs. "Mr. Mayor, since this is the prankster who ruined your party, why don't you do the honors?"

"I'd be glad to," the mayor said as he pulled off the clown's wig and mask.

"Ebenezer Bleezer!" exclaimed Uncle Walt.

Suddenly another police officer emerged from the kitchen leading someone in handcuffs. It was the waiter that Scooby and Shaggy had followed into the kitchen earlier during that party.

They could now see that he had been wearing a mask, and Fred pulled it off.

"Frank! I can't believe it!" Uncle Walt said faintly.

"Just as we thought," Velma said.

"Wow kids, I'm impressed," the mayor said, "How did you know?"

"It was difficult," Daphne said, "There were a few people hanging around the store who had something to gain by the Giggle Spot failing, and the piece of purple fuzz we found in the stockroom linked all of them to the thefts."

"But after finding more clues, we realized that there wasn't enough evidence to suggest that our culprit was the anti-prank activist — her purple fuzzy scarf was just a coincidence." Fred said,

"That left Ebeneezer Bleezer and Frank the Prank," Daphne added.

"Bleezer had the most motive, but he couldn't do it alone — he needed the help of someone who knew the Giggle spot inside and out — Frank the Prank. When we found the french fry in the stock room, we began to suspect that Frank had something to do with the missing items, but what really gave it away was when we found the map of the Giggle Spot. Frank wouldn't have needed it, but Bleezer certainly would have." Velma explained.

"Once he had the map, Bleezer snuck into the party dressed like that creepy clown so he could prank us all," Daphne said.

"And, like, Frank the Prank dressed like a waiter to get Scoob and me back to the kitchen," Shaggy added.

"That's right," said Frank the Prank. "Bleezer promised to make me the manager of my own Laugh Arcade franchise if I helped him sabotage the Giggle Spot. It was an offer I couldn't refuse."

"With Frank's help, I was going to take over Walt's business. I knew he had a maze of rooms under the Giggle Spot, all hiding secret gags!" Bleezer said, squirming as the police held his arms.

"Secret gags?" Velma turned to Uncle Walt. "What is he talking about?"

"This store has been in my family for a very long time. My grandfather was a magician. My father was an inventor, and he hid a secret prank vault under the Giggle Spot."

"I had everything planned out perfectly, and I would have gotten away with it if it weren't for these pesky kids!" Bleezer shouted as the police led him and Frank the Prank away.

"I don't know how to thank you kids enough," Uncle Walt said to the gang. "And you, too, Mr. Mayor. Your party saved my store."

"Like, now that we caught the prankster, can we eat?" Shaggy asked.

"The party leftovers!" Uncle Walt said.

Scooby and Shaggy licked their lips as Daphne

and Velma carried out the birthday cake and trays of sandwiches and appetizers. The gang ate every last crumb.

"Ruh Roh," Scooby said after everyone had finished.

"What's wrong now, Scoob?" Fred asked.

"Rungry," Scooby said, rubbing his belly.

"You're still hungry?" Velma asked.

"Like, here you go, Scoob," Shaggy said. "I found this can of snacks for you."

Shaggy handed Scooby a large can marked SNAX.

Scooby licked his chops again. He peeled open the can lid and a bunch of rubber snakes shot out, knocking him to the floor.

Everyone laughed. Shaggy laughed the hardest. He fell over onto the floor, too, grabbing at his sides.

"S-S-Sorry, Scoob," Shaggy said. He couldn't stop laughing. "I promise. I won't play any more jokes on you."

"Rake ron it?" Scooby asked.

Shaggy stood up. "Sure thing, Scoob." He held out his hand as Scooby extended his paw.

Zzzzzzzzzap!

Shaggy jumped back. Scooby had been hiding an electric hand buzzer in his paw.

Now Scooby was the one laughing. "Scooby-Dooby-Doo!"